THIS BOOK BELONGS TO:

. . . .

DATE DUE

DEC 1 9 2012	
JAN 0 2 2013	

DEMCO, INC. 38-2931

For my wife, Louise, who told me about the Little Reindeer

Other books by
MICHAEL FOREMAN:

Norman's Ark

Cat and Canary

Can't Catch Me!

Cat on the Hill

Dinosaur Time

One World

Peter's Place

War and Peas

Seal Surfer

First published in Great Britain in 1996 by Andersen Press Ltd., 20 Vauxhall Bridge Road, London SW1V 2SA.
This paperback edition first published in 2006 by Andersen Press Ltd.
Published in Australia by Random House Australia Pty., Level 3, 100 Pacific Highway, North Sydney, NSW 2060.
Copyright © Michael Foreman, 1996
The rights of Michael Foreman to be identified as the author and illustrator of this work have been asserted by him in accordance with the Copyright, Designs and Patents Act, 1988.
All rights reserved. Colour separated in Italy by Fotoriproduzioni, Grafiche, Verona. Printed and bound in Italy by Grafiche AZ, Verona.

10 9 8 7 6 5 4 3

British Library Cataloguing in Publication Data available.

ISBN 978 1 84270 582 7
This book has been printed on acid-free paper

THE LITTLE REINDEER

MICHAEL FOREMAN

Andersen Press • London

THE little reindeer wondered what all the fuss was about.
He could see lights blazing in the windows of the snow
covered buildings. Shadowy figures rushed in and out of
doorways carrying mysterious bundles.

The little reindeer picked his way through the deep snow towards the biggest building. As he got closer he could hear singing and banging, whirring and rustling.
The little reindeer peeped round the door into the warm, noisy room.

Amazing animals were streaming between rows of singing people. The little reindeer moved further into the room and suddenly found himself being carried along amongst the rest of the animals.

He tried to back away but was pushed forwards by the animals pressing from behind. Suddenly they all disappeared in a blizzard of coloured paper.

He was turned over and over in swirling colours. Then it went black and cold and things bumped down on him until he couldn't move.

He heard jingling bells and
cheering and he felt a great whoosh.

For hours they seemed to stop and start and swoop up and down until he was tumbling head over hoofs again.

He tried to move his legs, and managed to stand up. Although he was relieved to feel the softness of snow beneath his hoofs, he still couldn't see anything. The little reindeer stood in the darkness, surrounded by strange sounds. Then he heard footsteps crunching towards him.

Suddenly he found himself staring at an astonished face, and then a smile.

"Wow! What a present!" The boy picked him up and danced round and round in the snow.

"But where can I keep you? There are no pets allowed in the building. I know… You can stay up here with my pigeons."
    The boy opened the door of a large shed at one end of the roof. Immediately the sky filled with birds.

In a corner of the shed
the boy made a straw bed for
the reindeer and fetched milk
and a whole assortment of cereals.
"Tomorrow we can try lots of different
things to eat and see which you like best."
Two by two the pigeons returned to their
perches. They didn't seem to mind the
new visitor.

Each day the boy brought food and milk. The reindeer liked peanut butter sandwiches best of all. While the pigeons flew higher and higher in the sky, the boy and the reindeer strolled around the roof and watched the busy city life below.

The weather gradually grew warmer and the little reindeer grew bigger.

One day when the boy opened the door to let the pigeons out, the reindeer flew out with them.

The reindeer didn't fly far, that first
time, just across to the neighbouring
building and back. But as the days
passed, he flew further and further.
    The boy was overjoyed.
He had told no one about
his wonderful Christmas pet
because he knew he would not
be allowed to keep him.

By early summer the reindeer was big enough to give the boy rides around the roof on his back. Then, one evening, they flew together over the roofs of the city.

They flew together every night of the long summer
and over the golden leaves of autumn.

When the first snowflakes of winter
began to fall, the boy noticed a look
of sadness in the reindeer's eyes.
The boy hugged him as always, but
the reindeer looked up at the swiftly
moving grey clouds and sighed.

The boy knew that only six or
seven very special reindeer can
fly in each generation. He even
knew their names.
    He knew his reindeer was going
to be one of those very special ones.

On Christmas Eve the boy gave the reindeer his favourite dinner and the pigeons sang. They were still singing when he kissed the reindeer goodnight.

From his bed, he thought he heard jingling bells,
but he was probably dreaming by then.

Next morning he rushed up to the
roof but the reindeer had gone. There
were sleigh tracks in the snow. When
he opened the shed and all the pigeons
flew out the boy saw that each had a
red ribbon collar and a little jingle bell.
In the reindeer's bed of straw was a note -
  "Dear Boy,
       Thank you for looking after my
smallest reindeer. See you next year.
  Love,
    Santa Claus."

Through the next spring, summer and autumn the boy heard
the tinkling and jingling of bells each time the pigeons flew.
And on Christmas Eve, when he heard the real jingle bells
coming down from the snowy sky, he was waiting on the
roof with milk and peanut butter sandwiches.